Bath • New York • Cologne • Melbourne • Delhi
Hong Kong • Shenzhen • Singapore

*Rapunzel loves looking out over the Kingdom of Corona.*

Sketch
the view
from her
bedroom
window.

SOMEONE IS ABOUT TO FEEL THE WEIGHT OF RAPUNZEL'S FRYING PAN!

Draw who it might be.

Rapunzel enjoys sketching the people she sees around the village.

DOODLE SOME
FACES HERE.

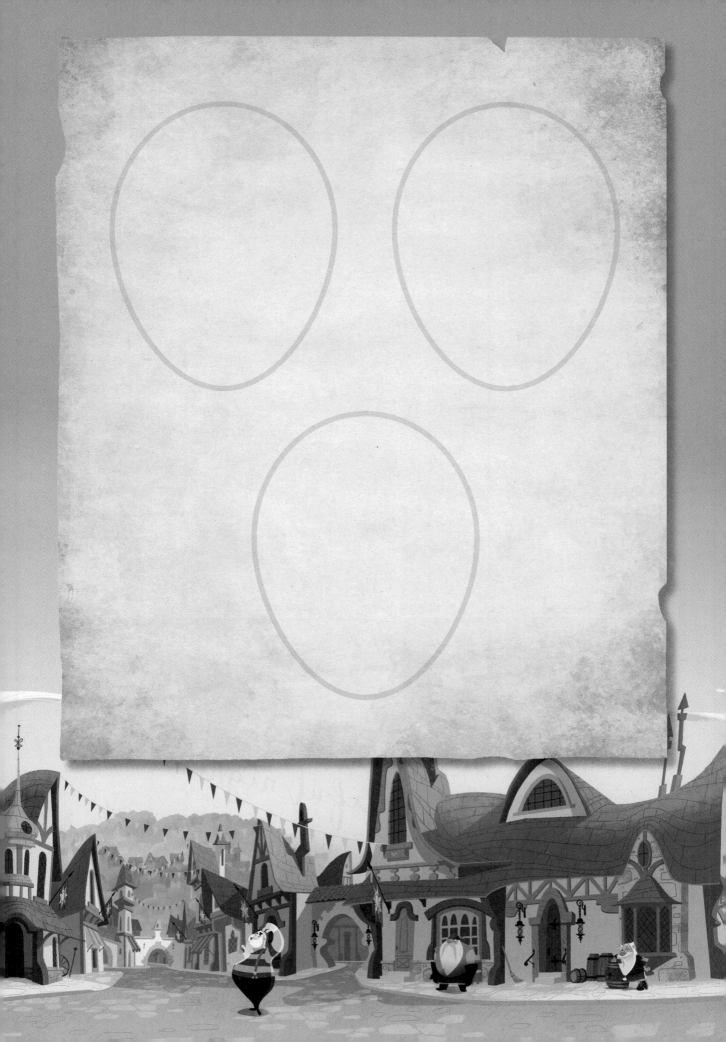

"It's a beautiful night.

Fill the sky above Rapunzel and Eugene with lots of twinkling stars.

# Rapunzel and Cassandra are exploring the forest.

DRAW TALL TREES ALL AROUND THEM.

Pascal has challenged
Rapunzel to a game of chess!

ADD THE PIECES TO THE BOARD.

There's a royal banquet at the castle.

FILL THE TABLE WITH
A FEAST OF DELICIOUS FOODS.

# Rapunzel longs to explore beyond the castle walls.

Doodle the world that awaits her.

# Rapunzel is going on an adventure.

DRAW ALL THE ITEMS
SHE WILL NEED FOR HER ADVENTURE KIT.

CASS HAS A PET OWL CALLED . . . OWL.

Draw an owl's-eye view looking down
on the beautiful Kingdom of Corona.

"Varian is an alchemist, a master of creating mysterious experiments.

# FILL HIS WORKBENCH WITH ALL SORTS OF AWESOME POTIONS.

Oops! Ruddiger
has knocked over
a bottle!

# IT'S SNOWING IN CORONA!

SKETCH LOTS OF SPARKLING SNOWFLAKES, AND MAKE EACH ONE DIFFERENT.

# mmm, cupcakes!

DOODLE A
DIFFERENT DECORATION
ON EACH DELICIOUS TREAT.

The queen has hung a few of Rapunzel's paintings on the palace walls.

SKETCH SOMETHING SPECTACULAR INSIDE EACH FRAME.

# SOME BAD GUYS HAVE ARRIVED IN CORONA, AND THEY'RE IN DISGUISE!

TO HIDE YOUR FACE, DESIGN A MASK HERE.

# WHEEEEE!

PASCAL IS USING RAPUNZEL'S HAIR AS A SLIDE.
SKETCH THE CHAMELEON WHIZZING BY.

THE KING, QUEEN, AND RAPUNZEL ARE PROTECTED BY THE ROYAL GUARD.

Draw a row of brave soldiers
standing beside the Captain of the Guard.

Lady Crowley
is always
scowly.

Sketch something funny to make her smile!

*Reading is one of Rapunzel's favorite hobbies.*

DRAW STACKS OF BOOKS FOR RAPUNZEL TO ENJOY.

# Rapunzel hardly ever wears shoes.

Fill the page with her footprints.

SKETCH A PILE OF BIG, JUICY APPLES
FOR MAXIMUS TO MUNCH ON.

Apples are his favorite food!

*Eugene can't help but admire himself in every shiny surface.*

DRAW HIS HANDSOME REFLECTION.

Eugene loves taking Rapunzel boating on the lake.

FILL THE WATER WITH

COLORFUL FISH.

Cassandra is practicing her sword fighting.

DRAW THE PERSON SHE IS TESTING HER SKILLS ON.

# Corona looks beautiful at sunset.

COLOR THE SKY IN FIERY REDS, YELLOWS, AND ORANGES.

Varian has been experimenting again.

Doodle the EXPLOSIVE results.

Draw
something
**spectacular**
on the easel.

Rapunzel
loves to
paint.

Rapunzel has been learning archery,
but is she any good?
Add arrows to the targets.

# ADD A BACKGROUND BEHIND EACH PICTURE OF PASCAL, AND THEN COLOR HIM SO HE BLENDS RIGHT IN!

# WHAT HAS CASSANDRA SPOTTED IN THE DARK?

Sketch something emerging from the shadows.

What a view!

Add details to the scene,
from birds in the sky to boats on the water.

# RAPUNZEL is a FEARLESS RIDER!

Draw lots of obstacles for Maximus to jump over.

# Rapunzel's bedroom is beautiful.

SKETCH IT, FROM HER BED
TO HER BOOKSHELVES.

# RAPUNZEL LOVES TO LOSE HERSELF IN A GOOD BOOK.

*Design some* **exciting** *book covers.*

# RAPS AND HER FRIENDS HAVE BUILT A HUGE SNOWMAN!

Draw their creation below,
and give it a big carrot nose.

# WHEN RAPUNZEL TOUCHED THE BLACK ROCK, THERE WAS

# AN EXPLOSION!

FILL THE PAGE WITH THE SHARP SPIKES BURSTING OUT EVERYWHERE.

# RAPUNZEL IS DECORATING THE CITY WALLS.

Help her finish the mural.

# THE PUB THUGS ARE HAVING A SING-ALONG!

## Fill the page with musical notes.

# Rapunzel's journal is filled with sketches.

## DRAW WHATEVER'S AROUND YOU RIGHT NOW.

# THE ROYAL FAMILY HAD A PORTRAIT PAINTED.

# DRAW YOUR OWN FAMILY PORTRAIT IN THE FRAME.

Vladimir collects *ceramic unicorns!*

DOODLE THE MOST *magical* UNICORN FOR HIM HERE.

# Pascal is hiding on the royal throne.

# Design a grand throne for yourself.

# THIS MAP SHOWS THE KINGDOM OF Corona.

CREATE A MAP OF THE AREA WHERE YOU LIVE.
MAKE SURE YOU MARK THE LOCATION OF YOUR HOME!

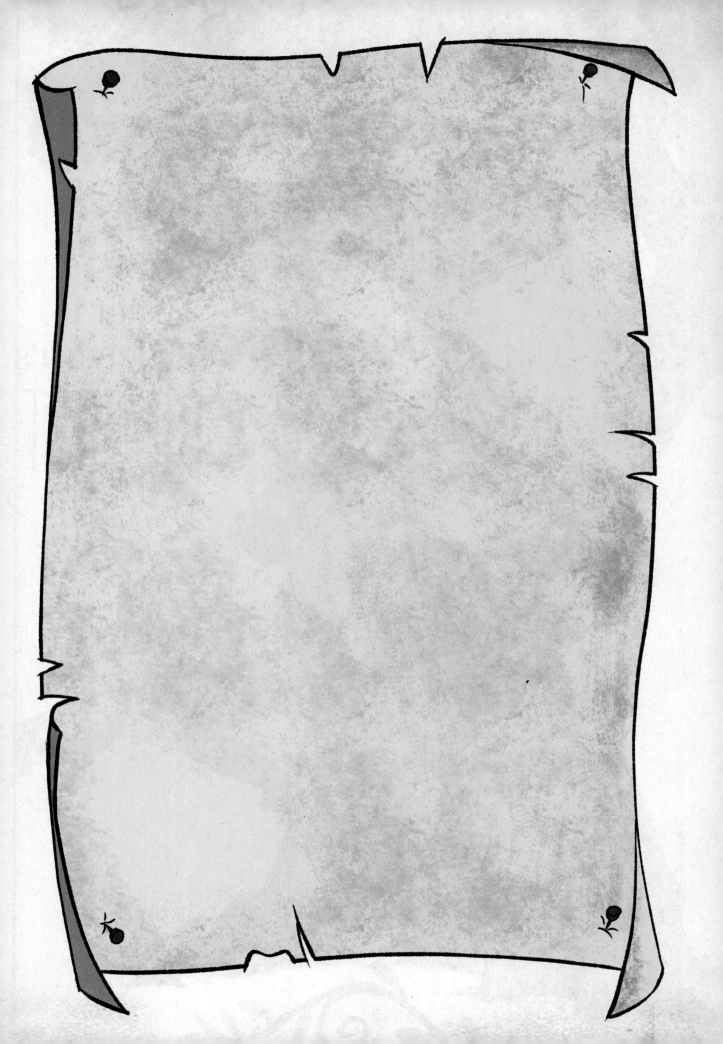

What is Cassandra's **BIGGEST** *secret*?

DOODLE A PICTURE OF IT.

Yee-haw!

Eugene swings into action.

DRAW RAPUNZEL
SWINGING BY HER HAIR,
READY TO JOIN
THE ADVENTURE.

THE CITY BULLETIN BOARD IS FILLED WITH ADS FOR ANYTHING AND EVERYTHING.

# RACE TIME!

DRAW THE SCENERY BEHIND RAPS AND EUGENE, AS THEY PASS BY IN A BLUR.

# RUDDIGER IS ALWAYS LOOKING FOR HIS NEXT SNACK.

FILL THE PAGE WITH HEALTHY FRUIT AND VEGETABLES FOR HIM TO EAT.

*Best pals Rapunzel and Pascal are playing around.*

Draw the log Rap is balancing on, and a stream beneath it.

ADD A DESIGN TO THE BIG LANTERNS, BEFORE THEY FLOAT INTO THE SKY.

It's celebration time in Corona!
Fill the page with banners and flags.

Rapunzel's golden locks are looping all around the page. Draw her hair!

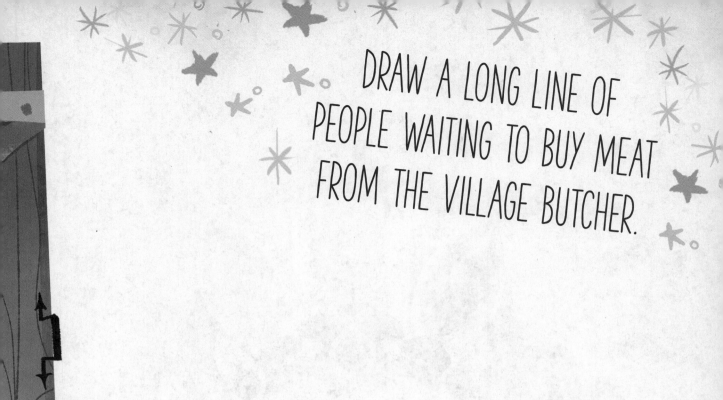

DRAW A LONG LINE OF PEOPLE WAITING TO BUY MEAT FROM THE VILLAGE BUTCHER.

# RAPUNZEL'S TIARA GLITTERS WITH JEWELS.

*Design your own tiara. . . .*

WILL IT BE
GOLD OR SILVER?

WHAT COLOR STONES
WILL YOU CHOOSE?

# RAPUNZEL WANTS TO SNEAK OUT OF THE CASTLE, SO SHE'S TRYING ON SOME DISGUISES.

Draw her in a funny costume.

# WHAT CAN PASCAL SEE THROUGH THE TELESCOPE?

Doodle the magical midnight view.

Eugene used to be known as Flynn Rider, when he was a thief.

Add his face to the WANTED poster— and try to get his nose right!

# CASSANDRA'S WARDROBE IS FILLED WITH . . .
## WEAPONS!

Sketch more swords, maces, and axes for her collection.

Rapunzel has set up a bowl of fruit for a still-life painting.

SEE IF YOU CAN DRAW THE PLATE OF DELICIOUSNESS HERE.

# The castle gateway doesn't have a door.
## DESIGN ONE HERE!

The royal family is HUNGRY!

DRAW THE KING,

QUEEN, AND RAPUNZEL SITTING IN THE CHAIRS.

Roses are red. . . . .

Design a vase for these beautiful blooms.

Now draw a big bouquet of flowers
for Eugene to give to Rapunzel.

WHAT'S TICKLING EUGENE?
DRAW SOMETHING FUNNY HERE.

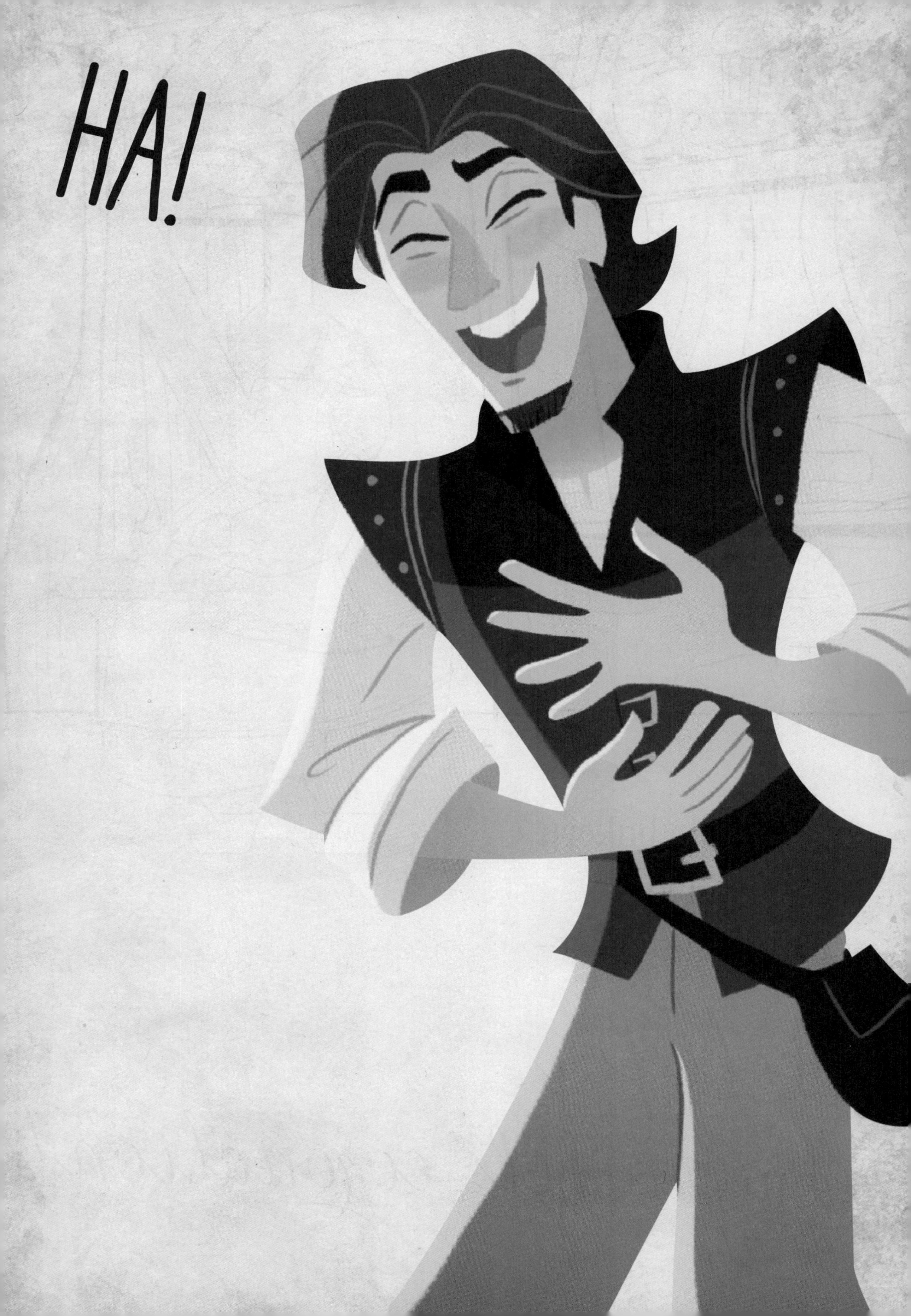
HA!

The village bakery
has a VERY
important order—

a cake for
Rapunzel's coronation!

Design a cake fit for a royal occasion.

Raps has found an overgrown grove. Draw things that have remained hidden here for years. . . .

Rapunzel wears colorful flowers in her long hair.

DRAW LOTS OF BLOOMS ALONG HER LOCKS.

RAPUNZEL WOULD LOVE TO PAINT THIS PEACEFUL SCENE!

For her coronation,
Rapunzel will wear
a **HUGE** wig!

Doodle more hairstyle
options for the
princess-to-be.

It's the perfect night for a moonlit ride.

SKETCH THE SILHOUETTES OF RAPUNZEL AND EUGENE ON THEIR HORSES.

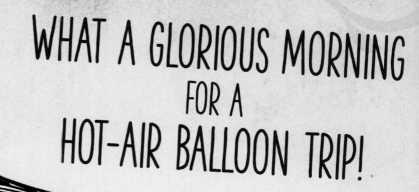

WHAT A GLORIOUS MORNING
FOR A
HOT-AIR BALLOON TRIP!

Fill the sky with lots of colorful balloons.

WHAT IS EACH MEMBER OF THE ROYAL FAMILY THINKING ABOUT?

DRAW THEIR THOUGHTS!

# Fidella is ready for bed.

DESIGN A STABLE FOR HER TO REST IN.

Hook Foot loves to dance!

Draw a stage for him to perform on,
and then sketch him mid-twirl.

RAPUNZEL IS POSING
FOR EUGENE, WHO WANTS
TO LEARN TO PAINT LIKE HER.

UNFORTUNATELY, HE'S NOT VERY GOOD YET. . . . .
DOODLE HIS ATTEMPT TO CAPTURE RAPS ON CANVAS.

SOMETIMES SHORTY LIKES TO BE EUGENE'S SIDEKICK.

# DRAW THE TWO OF THEM
# ON A CRAZY ADVENTURE TOGETHER.

# Rapunzel is preparing to get creative.

Surround her
with brushes
and pots of paint.

# Eugene has had many adventures over the years.

## WHO OR WHAT IS HE RUNNING AWAY FROM?

Splish
splash
splash!

Fill the page with colorful splashes of paint.

# Splish, splash, splosh!

Fill the page with colorful splats of paint.

# Eugene loves the royal life.

## DRAW PILES OF FOOD FOR HIM TO EAT.

THIS SUN SHAPE APPEARS ALL AROUND CORONA.

DRAW IT AS MANY
TIMES AS YOU CAN.

ULF IS A MIME ARTIST
WHO NEVER SAYS A WORD.

SKETCH HIM MIMING
SOMETHING WITH HIS BODY.

The king adores his princess-to-be, Rapunzel.

DRAW THE ROYAL CASTLE BEHIND THEM.

Cass doesn't like painting
very much. . . .

# DRAW HER DOING SOMETHING SHE ENJOYS!

OWL COMES
OUT TO PLAY
AT NIGHT.

ADD HIM
PERCHED ON
THE BRANCH.

Now draw some other creatures that come out at night.

Eugene wants to marry Rapunzel and
he's practicing his proposal on Maximus.

DRAW THE HORSE LOOKING LESS THAN IMPRESSED!

CASS IS A TOP SHOT.

DRAW TODAY'S TARGET.

RAPS HAS A SPARKLING TIARA FOR HER CORONATION. WHAT OTHER JEWELRY WILL SHE WEAR?

Fill the page with more jewels for her to pick from.

Eugene has chosen a *diamond ring* for Rapunzel.

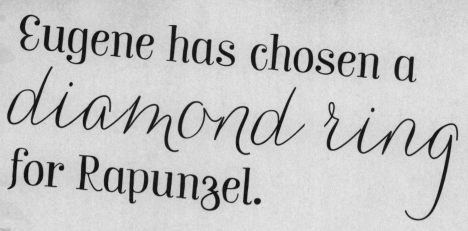

# Draw the ring on Rapunzel's hand!

SKETCH YOURSELF SITTING AT RAPUNZEL'S DESK, READY TO WRITE OR DRAW.

Rapunzel has so many paintbrushes!

DRAW MORE HERE.

Now add your favorite colors to the paint palette.

Rapunzel is so loved in Corona that she has her own statue!

# Draw yourself as a statue below.

# RAPS NEEDS MORE SPACE TO STORE ALL OF HER BOOKS.

## DRAW ANOTHER BOOKCASE OR SOME SHELVES FOR HER.

THE CORONA DUNGEON IS A **DARK** AND **SCARY** PLACE.

Who's been thrown in jail?

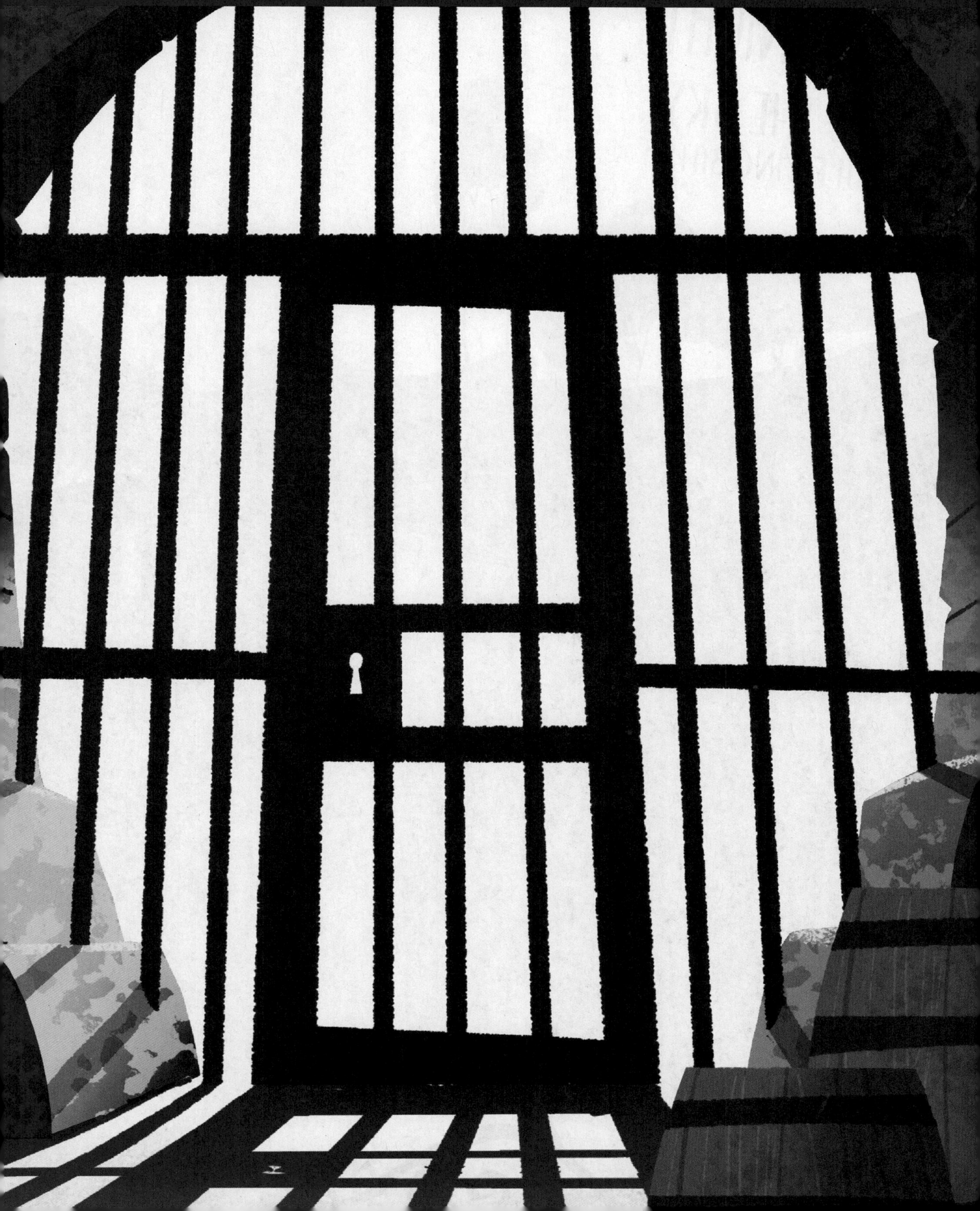

# IT'S A
# DARK NIGHT.

## FILL THE SKY
### WITH FLYING BATS.

# THE KINGDOM OF CORONA HAS MANY STORES.

*Complete this village scene.*

The royal castle is full of secrets.
What's behind the big locked doors?

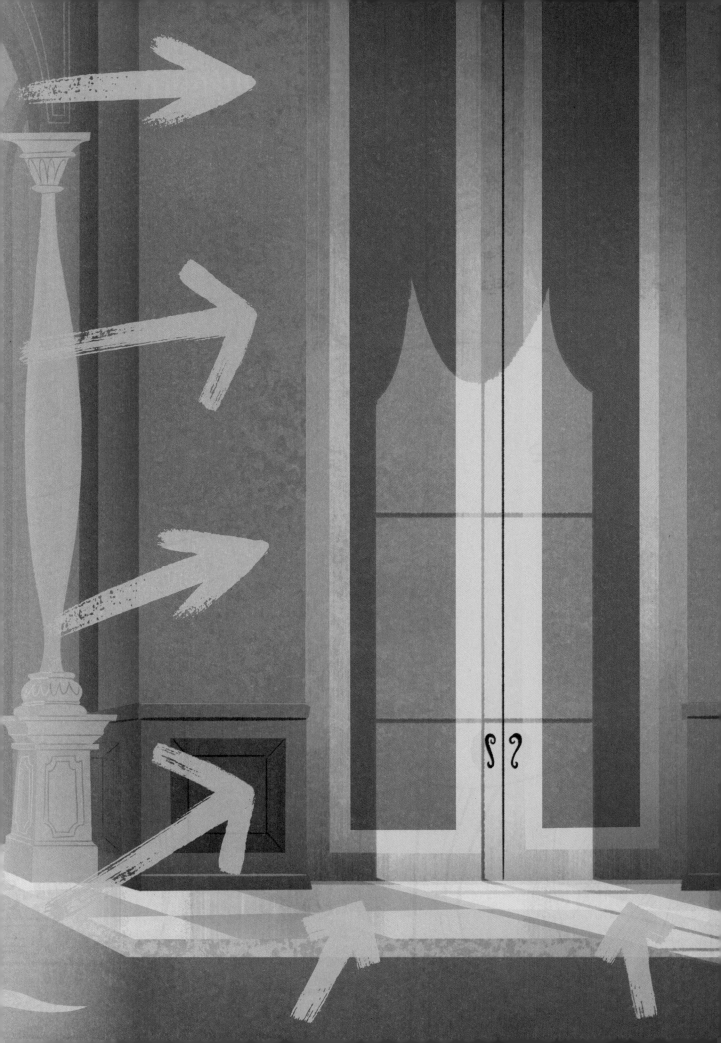

Rapunzel is daydreaming. Doodle her thoughts.

RAPUNZEL HAS PAINTED A PRETTY PATTERN.

FINISH THE DESIGN FOR HER.

Queen Arianna has had some beautiful shoes made for Rapunzel to wear at her coronation.

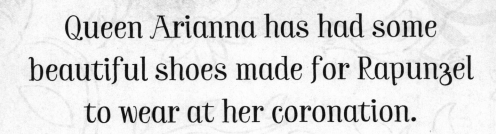

DESIGN THEM HERE!

Now if only Raps would wear them. . . .

Pascal is having a tea party!

# WHO IS HIS GUEST?

*Hopefully they'll be big enough to lift the teapot....*

People have started to arrive for Rapunzel's coronation.

DRAW TWO CARRIAGES BRINGING THE GUESTS TO THE CASTLE.

# Rapunzel's bedroom is filled with lanterns.

Draw more hanging from the ceiling.

PASCAL IS SHOWING OFF HIS COLOR-CHANGE TRICK.

COLOR THE CUSHIONS SO HE BLENDS IN.

# CASSANDRA WAS RAISED IN THE CASTLE AND IS RAPUNZEL'S LADY-IN-WAITING.

*She is also a skilled fighter and acts as Rapunzel's guard.*

# Draw Cass in her adventurer's outfit, so she feels more comfortable.

# LADY CAINE AND THE RAT
# MAKE A WICKED TEAM.

## DRAW A PICTURE OF YOU WITH YOUR BEST BUDDY.

RAIN OR SHINE, RAPUNZEL LOVES BEING IN THE GREAT OUTDOORS!

ADD THE SUN AND A RAINBOW TO THIS WET-WEATHER SCENE.

*Rapunzel often paints woodland creatures in her murals.*

ADD MORE ANIMALS TO THE PAGE.

IT'S A BUSY DAY IN THE KINGDOM OF CORONA.
FILL THE STREETS WITH PEOPLE!

Big Nose loves to write poems and then share them.

Give him an audience!

# ATTILA DREAMS OF OPENING A BAKERY.

## HIS STRAWBERRY PUFFS ARE DIVINE!

Draw your favorite
sweet treat here.

It's a summer's day and the butterflies are stretching their wings.

FILL THE PAGE WITH MORE FLYING CREATURES.

RAPUNZEL WOULD RATHER BE ADVENTURING THAN PRINCESSING.

Sketch her sitting on Max,
ready to gallop off in search of excitement.